four magic words

written by Elisa Solea

First Published in 2020
Copyright text © Elisa Solea
Copyright illustrations © Elisa Solea
All rights reserved
ISBN: 978-9925-7678-1-6

www.urmagicalkids.net

dedicated to Kiana

Author's Acknowledgements

This book was created with love and with environmental consciousness. We ensure that we are doing our
part to protect the environment.
A portion of the proceeds from this book is being donated to Tree Planting.

four magic words

The book belongs to

and was created with love

Activities for parents and teachers to develop imagination and speech as well as emotional intelligence.

While you read the book you will see some numbers. Each number represents an activity listed below. Enjoy your reading and most of all have fun!

Before you start reading the book, ask your children to guess the magic words. What is so special about specific words? Can they name any word that causes emotions, like I love you, I am happy, I am upset, hurray! Etc. Play the mirror game. Do faces in front of a mirror with them – happy, sad, angry, surprised, etc. it helps to strengthen their facial muscles needed for speaking as well as to help them get in touch with their feelings and emotions.

Ask your children to count up to a number they know. Then tell them to count backwards. Ask them to find five objects in the room that are bigger or smaller than two cm. Through this, children will start getting a sense of size.

Ask your children about the last time they were upset. What made them feel that way? Can they empathize with the woodman? When they are feeling upset and sad, what makes them feel better? Share a moment when you were upset and how you have overcome it.

Imagination time. Let your children guess what happens at the end of the story. How did the woodman become so small? What could be the cause? Can he become big again and return home?

Ask your children how they feel when someone shouts or talks abruptly to them. Explain to them that this is how the fairy feels right now. Now ask them to remember a moment where they were shouting at someone else (siblings, parents, friends), what made them so upset? Can they relate with the other person they were shouting at? Is it worth it to make someone feel that way? So let's try to be more calm next time we have these feelings.

Try to explain to the children about the law of attraction (you can find guidelines and more info on www.urmagicalkids.net. The universe always listens, you just need to ask clearly, and you shall receive.

Trees teach, offer and protect. Ask the children to give examples on each word. What can trees teach us? What do they offer us? How do they protect us? Trees absorb carbon dioxide and release the valuable oxygen we need to breathe.

Trees can reduce air temperature and wind speed. Trees absorb and block noise and dust and reduce glare. Trees create an ecosystem to provide habitat and food to birds and other animals. An inspiring book on trees is "Lomax" by Dr. Seuss and "The Book of Trees" by Piotr Socha and Wojciech Grajkowski.

 Game. Ask the children which are our five senses. Play with them the game of senses. Ask them to close their eyes. Start with the hearing. What noises can they hear? Touch. Give them objects with various textures. Can they feel the difference? Can they recognize the objects without looking? Smell. What smells can they pick up? Does a specific smell remind them of something? Can they differentiate various smells, etc.

 Ask them if they have a favorite fairytale. Why did they choose the specific one? Was it because they liked the story or the hero? Do they identify with the hero and why? Who is their favorite writer? When they read a book, do they check who wrote it? Do they have various books of a specific writer?

 Ask the children if they get what the fairy is trying to say. Is it possible for two people to look at the same thing and see something completely different? Can they think of a way to prove their point?

 Draw on a piece of paper the number 6. Show it to them. Then turn the page upside down to show number 9. Ask them again what number they see. Explain that even though they look at the same drawing, they see something different just by turning the page upside down. So next time they are very sure about something, they should look at the bigger picture instead of trying to prove they are right. Whatever we hear and say is just an opinion, not a fact. Whatever we see is just a visual not the truth!

 Fear. What is their biggest fear? Why do they feel insecure? Whatever the children share with you, accept it and hug them. Discuss with them and find ways together so they can conquer their fears.

 The fairy hugged the tree. Explain to the children the therapeutic energy of tree hugging. Arrange on your next outing to hug the first tree you find. More info on tree hugging on the website www.urmagicalkids.net

 The magic words "I'm sorry, please forgive me, thank you and I love you" why do you think have so much power? Discuss it with your children and say it out loud to each other.

Once upon a time there was a woodman. Every day the woodman went deep in the dense green forest to cut wood. As he was about to cut a big tree, he was doused in a strange, glittering dust and began to shrink until he became as small as a 2cm pin.  He looked up and started panicking. The most beautiful tree that he wanted to cut looked enormous. It was so gigantic and imposing that it seemed as if it reached the sky. The woodman was very upset; 2

And now?

What is he going to do now? 3

While in despair, he heard a voice. "Have you ever considered how much these beautiful trees hurt every time you cut them without any hesitation?" yelled the voice. The woodman turned abruptly and he spied a bright fairy. She was the same size as him. The wings of the fairy sparkled with glitter, like the one he was doused in a few moments ago. "Did you shrink me?" shouted the woodman angrily. ⭐4 "I'm sorry... it was not on purpose, really. It's just when I saw you trying to cut this magnificent tree I got so furious that I wished that you become small, tiny just like me, so you can not hurt it anymore."

"So when you fairies wish for something, it comes
true?" doubtfully said the woodman.

"When you really want something, and believe in
it with your pure heart, then you can do everything.
That is the basic law of attraction". 5

"And you shrank me just to stop me from cutting
a tree?" the woodman demanded an answer.

"I did it because you haven't learned to respect
them. I see you every day coming into the forest
killing one tree after the other, without any
hesitation."

"Kill? Trees aren't alive!" he said with certainty.

"They're not alive? Can't you see how much life a
tree has, that from a tiny seed, it slowly produces 6
leaves and over time it grows until it becomes huge."

"Ok, but trees don't feel, they don't speak, which
means they don't have a soul."

The fairy was astonished "They don't have a soul?"
She forcefully pulled the woodman by the hand.

Close your eyes and listen carefully" she urged. 

The woodman, with his eyes closed, felt a light breeze on his cheek. He heard the wind passing through each leaf, it sounded like a beautiful melody. He was able to distinguish the steps of an army of ants that were vertically climbing the trunk of the tree and heard a bird sitting down to rest. The smell that filled the air trigger all his senses. Suddenly all senses were joined together and became one, the song of the soul. The woodman agreed "You are right. Now that I've realized my mistake, please

transform me again into a
normal man so I can go back
to my family?"
The fairy, being absolutely
satisfied with her achievement,
wished with all of her heart
that the woodman would turn
into a normal-sized person
again. She closed her eyes and
concentrated all her power
and then desperately wished
out loud.
"I would like my woodman to
become exactly as he was."
But nothing changed...
The woodman started to worry.
"What's wrong? Why doesn't
your wish come true?"

"I don't know. I really want it but I don't know why it's not working".

The woodman shuttered "And now what? Will I stay like this forever?"

"The only thing we can do is go to the Fairy Queen. She'll certainly know how to handle this," and the fairy started flying away in a panic.

"Hey! Where are you going?" yelled the woodman. "I can't fly!"

"Oh, I completely forgot that you don't have wings, sorry! Ok lets walk."

"You know we have been talking for so long and I still don't know your name" said the fairy.

"My name is Cyrus. What is yours?"

"They call me Kiana and I am the fairy of the elements of earth. Do you have any children, Cyrus?"

"Yes, I have two, a boy and a girl.

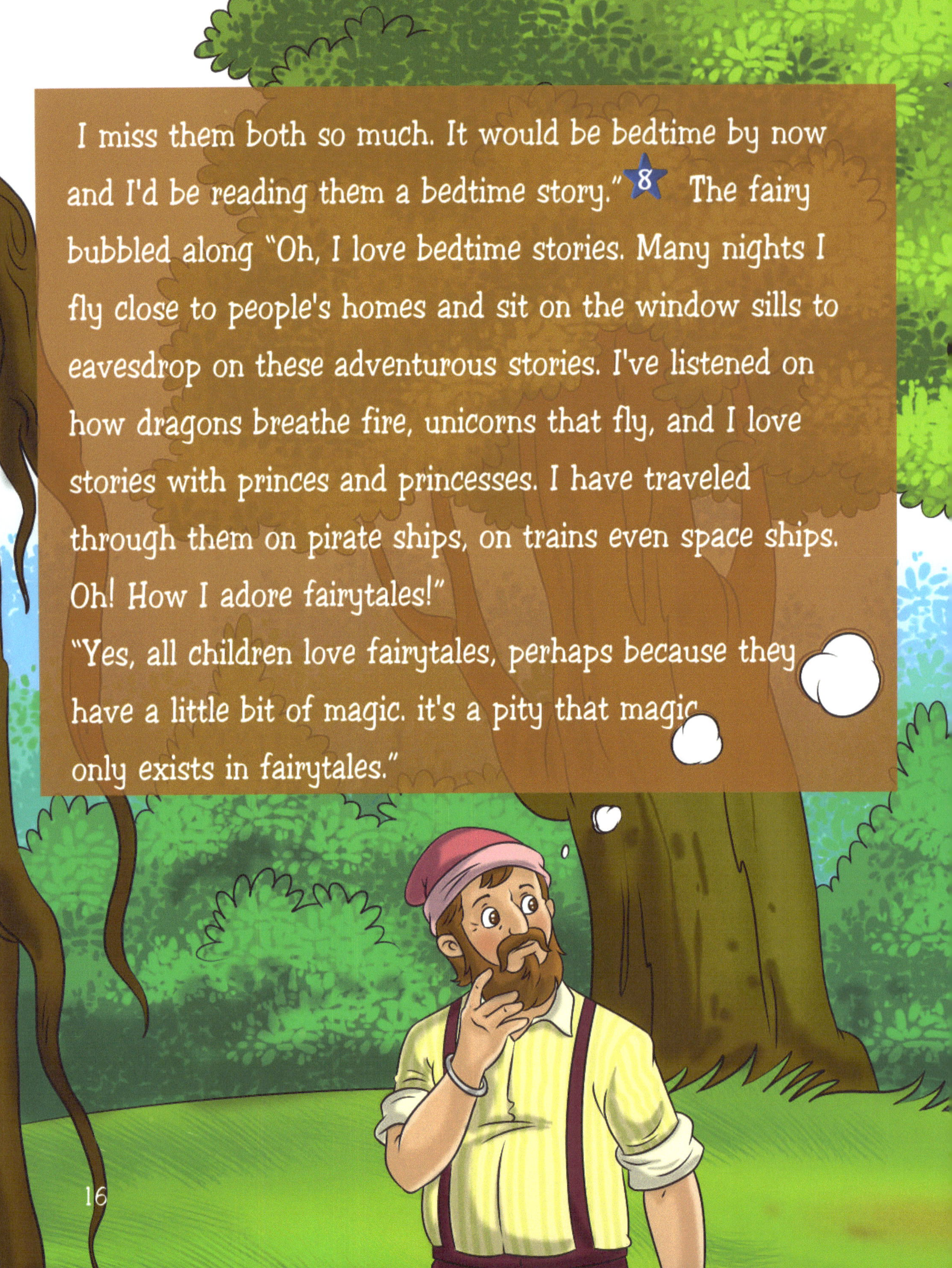

I miss them both so much. It would be bedtime by now and I'd be reading them a bedtime story." **8** The fairy bubbled along "Oh, I love bedtime stories. Many nights I fly close to people's homes and sit on the window sills to eavesdrop on these adventurous stories. I've listened on how dragons breathe fire, unicorns that fly, and I love stories with princes and princesses. I have traveled through them on pirate ships, on trains even space ships. Oh! How I adore fairytales!"

"Yes, all children love fairytales, perhaps because they have a little bit of magic. it's a pity that magic only exists in fairytales."

"Only exists in fairytales? Magic is everywhere, anything can happen." emphasized the fairy.

"You sound like small children that believe in stories" teased the woodman.

"And why is it bad to believe in fairytales? How do you know that those stories aren't real? All stories have an amount of truth in them based on each one's perspective." ⭐9

"What are you talking about? We all see the same things. There are no two truths," said the woodman in disbelief.

The fairy took some stones and formed the number six on the ground.

"What do you see?" she asked the woodman.

"Well number nine," answered the woodman in certainty.

"Are you sure you see this number ? What if I tell you that I see something else? Would I be wrong?"

"Definitely," declared the woodman.

"Then come to my side and tell me what I am looking at. Now you see what I see, the number six. We both tell the truth, we just see the same thing from a different ankle. So even though we are both telling the truth, we have a different story to tell." 10

The woodman started getting tired. "What about taking a nap for a while? I need to rest my eyes."

"Oh my" said the fairy really scared "The flowers have already closed their petals, where are we going to find shelter?"

The woodman tried to sooth her "We can lay here by the trunk of this tree. Don't be afraid, I will be here for you."

The woodman and the fairy lied and covered themselves with some leaves and fell asleep.

In the morning the fairy hugged and thanked the tree for hosting them. The woodman got up and started walking. 12

"Hey!" yelled the fairy. "Aren't you going to thank it, too?"

"Why? Does the tree understand me?"

"So you need to be ungrateful? The tree offered us a roof and warmness for the night and you find it difficult to say thank you? You should know that when you appreciate those offering to you then nothing is pointless."

The fairy was right; these trees were his whole life. With tears in his eyes he hugged the tree with his tiny hands, as hard as he could and sobbed, "I am sorry, please forgive me, thank you, I love you." 13

I am
sorry, please forgive me,
thank you, I love you.

That moment, a glistening shiny beam filled the atmosphere and the woodman started getting bigger and bigger until he reached his normal size.

"But how did this happen?" the woodman stammered.

"We all have the power to achieve what we want. Magic is within. You succeeded in achieving what you wanted because you said the four magic words and you meant them."

The woodman kissed fairy Kiana and thanked her for all her help. Since then, every time the woodman cut a tree, he hugged it and thanked it for its offer to him and his family, and they all lived happily ever after.

About the Author
Elisa Solea is most importantly a mother. That is what triggered her to write
a Children's book, since before that she wrote and published four novels.
After she gave birth, she started to follow spirituality and a holistic way of life.
She studied Holistic Therapies and Child's psychology. She decided to write
a Children's book to help children evolve spiritually, mentally and
emotionally.
You can contact the author at
urmagicalkids@gmail.com
Elisa Solea

www.urmagicalkids.net

I will like to thank my husband Hadi Khalifeh
for helping and tolerating me, my father
Andreas Soleas for his creative feedback,
my sister Ioanna Soleas for the final touches
and my mother Luise for being who she is.
And of course my little inspiration Kiana.